Stars of the Red Carpet

Written by Marianne Posadas
Illustrated by Susy Boyer

Contents

NELSON CENGAGE Learning
For learning solutions, visit cengage.com.au

Meet the Characters

Eva Schiavoni

A city lawyer.

Tania Schiavoni

Eva's eleven-year-old daughter.

Steve

A tow-truck driver (among other things).

Myrtle

A bakery manager.

Dear Reader

Like many people, I lead a busy life. I'm always rushing here or there, and never seem to have a moment to myself. At the end of a busy day, I sometimes flop down on the couch and think how nice it would be to change

everything and have a relaxed, peaceful life. Here's a story about a busy family who felt the same way.

Marianne Posadas
Author

A Quiet Little Town

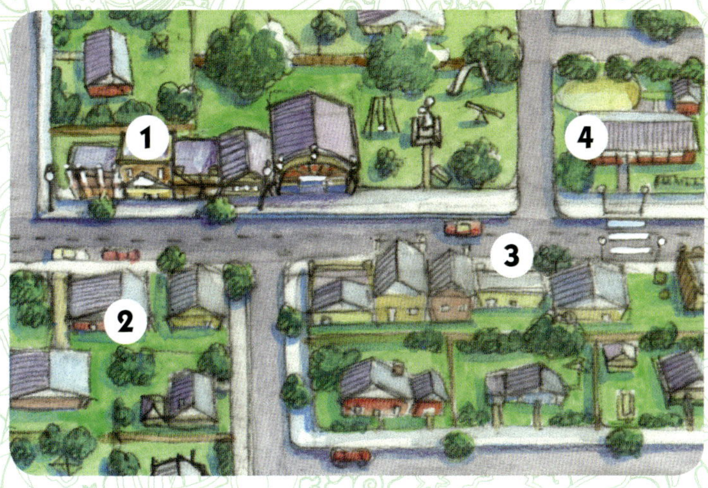

1. The Empire theatre
2. Steve's garage
3. Myrtle's bakery
4. The school

1 A Stressful Day

"That's it!" declared Tania's mother Eva, as she struggled awkwardly through the door of the apartment. "I've had enough!"

She slumped against the hallway wall. An ominous pool of water slowly spread out from the leather shoulder bag she had dumped unceremoniously on the floor. Her hair was wet and bedraggled. Her eye make-up was running down her face. Her expensive Italian suede shoes squelched like a pair of sodden thongs that someone had found drifting in a swimming pool.

Tania looked across at the spectacle that was her mother. She put down the knife she'd been using to slice vegetables for dinner and hurried into the hallway with a dry tea towel.

"How was your trip to Sydney?" she asked, handing her mother the tea towel. It had been quite a different scene earlier that day.

"Eva Schiavoni, entertainment lawyer, ready for action!" her mother had said, as the first rays of the sun had crept over their apartment balcony that morning. "How do I look?"

At that point, with her smart suit, careful make-up, perfectly styled hair and confident manner, Tania's mother had looked every bit like a Hollywood lawyer, ready to use her steely gaze to cut deals for the international movie chain she represented.

Now she looked more like she'd got a part in a Brollywood movie. Except they'd forgotten to give her the umbrella.

"Grrr!" said Eva from underneath the tea towel, as she furiously rubbed her hair dry. "Don't even ask me about that diabolical trip to Sydney, Tania! Grrr!"

Tania knew she wouldn't have to ask again. As soon as her mother had dried her hair, rubbed the ghoulish-looking mascara off her cheeks and found some dry clothes, Tania had little doubt that she would hear all about it.

Eva squelched off towards the bedroom, her shoes sounding like ducks quacking after a crust of bread floating downstream.

Tania finished slicing the vegetables and tidied up the kitchen bench, just in time for her mother's reappearance.

Eva pulled up a bar stool and rested her elbows dejectedly on the kitchen bench. "What a day!" she exclaimed, grabbing a carrot stick and talking and munching at the same time. "There was an incredible traffic jam on the freeway to the airport. No parking spots within kilometres of the terminal. Frustratingly long, winding check-in queues. I got the middle seat of the row – you know how much I hate that – and the flight attendant spilled orange juice on me as he was reaching across to fill people's glasses."

Tania's mother took a deep breath, and another carrot stick, then continued.

"Late taking off. Circled Sydney for hours because of air-traffic congestion. Another incredible traffic jam on the freeway into the city. Late for an important meeting about the new movie releases. Late for my flight home. Traffic jam on the way back to the airport. Huge check-in queues. Another middle seat, can you believe it? Bad weather delayed take-off. Bad weather delayed landing. Torrential rain floods the entire carpark where, of course, I've had to park right at the other end. Get soaked. Ticket too soggy to put in the parking machine. Finally get out, only to hit a traffic jam on the freeway into the city."

Eva looked at Tania, and waggled the last of her carrot in despair.

"It took me longer to drive home than it did for me to fly from Sydney. Can you believe that?"

"Sounds just like last Friday," said Tania, shaking her head. "I'm sorry you had such a stressful day, Mum."

"Anyway, that's it," declared Eva. "I've had enough of this ridiculous lifestyle. I'm supposed to go in to the office tomorrow morning and give a presentation on today's meeting, but I'm not going to."

"It's Saturday tomorrow," protested Tania. "You shouldn't have to go in to work on a Saturday."

"I'm not. I'm going to email in my report and, after I've finished that, you and I are going to spend some time together. Some relaxing time."

"That would be nice," smiled Tania. "You know, it's been a long time since we had a whole Saturday together, Mum."

“I’m going to email the office right now,” said Eva determinedly, “and then we’ll decide what to do with the weekend. *Our* weekend.”

Eva jumped off the bar stool and retrieved her laptop from the damp shoulder bag sitting on the hallway floor. She brought it back to the kitchen bench and lifted up the screen.

Tania watched from the other side of the bench as her mother pressed the power button. But instead of the usual log-in beep, the laptop let out a wheezy fizzle.

Eva peered at the laptop in dismay.

“Oh, dear,” said Tania.

Just to remove any lingering doubts about its condition, the laptop let out a tiny puff of steam.

“That’s it!” the wet laptop seemed to say. “I’ve had enough, too!”

2 A Drive in the Country

The last of Friday night's rain lay in stubborn pools at the edges of the concrete, defying the efforts of the morning sun to evaporate it.

Tania and her mother were eating toast on the balcony of their apartment, watching the traffic crawling beneath them. Every so often, the low hum of the cars was drowned out by the noise of a motorcycle racing impatiently past, or a siren urgently heading in the direction of some emergency. A helicopter clattered across the skyline and a reversing truck beeped insistently, flashing its orange lights like a gigantic, lumbering alarm clock.

"That's it," nodded Eva, wiping toast crumbs from the corner of her mouth. "That's what we'll do."

"A drive in the country," agreed Tania, collecting the breakfast dishes. "That would be a great way to spend the day, Mum."

"We'll just head south and see where the road takes us," said Eva. "It'll be an adventure, like two intrepid explorers venturing into the unknown and uncharted wilderness!"

Tania smiled and headed off to her room to pack a few essentials for the day's explorations.

Eva stood up and stretched her arms. An adventure was just what was needed to take her mind off her stressful lifestyle.

"But not too wilderness," she reassured herself. "Not too intrepid. There have to be at least a couple of lattes along the way."

"Ready?" called Eva.

"Ready!" replied Tania, hurrying out of her room.

Eva slung a bag over her shoulder, then hesitated. She'd spied her mobile phone on the kitchen bench. Should she take it?

Tania followed her gaze.

"Mum, it's our day," she pleaded. "If you take that,

you know you'll just be getting phone calls from the office all day."

Eva knew that would be true. Still, leaving home without the mobile was like leaving home without your wallet, handbag or shoes. It just couldn't be done.

"Tell you what," said Eva, picking up the phone and flicking through the options until she found what she wanted. "I've turned it to silent. That way we won't be bothered."

Tania nodded. It was a fair compromise – and she knew how much her mother hated being without her mobile phone.

Starting their trip without any definite plans and no particular place to go felt strangely rebellious to Eva. She and Tania had a simple system for choosing which roads to take. Eva was in charge of saying "right" and Tania was in charge of saying "left". They took it in turns to choose roads to take – and the person whose turn it was could choose any intersection, roundabout or set of traffic lights they wanted.

It wasn't long before they were far from the city, driving happily down an unfamiliar road neither of them had ever been on before.

"This is fun," beamed Eva.

"It sure is," agreed Tania. She hadn't seen her mother smile so much in ages. She wound down the window and breathed in the fresh country air. Eva even gave a friendly wave to drivers heading the other way, which was something that Tania had never seen her mother do in the city.

They stopped at a small town and, to their great delight, found a bakery. There, they bought delicious fresh bread rolls and an appetising-looking cake each to take along on their journey.

Eva was enjoying her Saturday so much she even forgot to order a latte.

"Doesn't matter," she said after they headed out of the town, accompanied by the delicious aroma of rolls and cakes wafting from the back seat. "We'll get one at the next place. In the meantime, let's keep driving and find a pleasant picnic spot to enjoy our lunch."

After about twenty minutes, they found a spot, sheltered by shady gum trees, where they could pull off the road and enjoy their rolls and cakes.

Eva parked the car, then Tania jumped out eagerly to stretch her legs. "There's even a picnic table," she called, pointing underneath the trees.

"Great," said Eva. "This is the kind of perfect Saturday that should just stretch out forever."

Little did Eva know that, by the end of the day, it would seem exactly like it was stretching out forever – and not in the way she expected.

The first sign of trouble arrived after Eva and Tania had finished their lunch. Inside the car, they buckled their seatbelts, looking forward to the next stage of their journey into the "wilderness".

Eva turned the key. Nothing happened.

"That's strange," frowned Eva. She tried again. This time the engine groaned, like someone in a deep sleep protesting about being shaken awake. Except the engine wasn't awake. It just rolled over and grunted as if it were pulling the blankets back over its head.

Tania looked at her mother.

"Don't worry," said Eva. "It's probably just overheated. It's been a while since this car's been anywhere except on a city freeway." But ten minutes later, with the engine still refusing to start, Eva's optimism began to fade. She felt around in her shoulder bag and found her mobile phone.

"Lucky I did bring this," she said, checking to see if there was any coverage. There was – and as confirmation, the phone blinked that there were seven text messages and three voice messages, all from the office. Eva ignored them and dialled directory.

It took the tow truck another hour to make it out to the spot where Eva and Tania waited patiently. It had taken three or four phone calls just to pinpoint exactly where they were, and the tow-truck driver from some town Eva had never heard of seemed in no hurry to come and rescue them.

Finally, however, with a loud gnashing of gears and a rumble of tyres, help arrived in the form of a rusty, dented tow truck rolling into the rest stop.

"Going Nowhere?" read the sign painted on the truck's battered back bumper. "Stick with Steve."

A man jumped energetically out of the truck's cab. He sauntered over to where Eva and Tania were leaning on their bonnet.

"Lovely day," he said cheerily, wiping a hand on his dirty overalls and holding it out to Eva. "I'm Steve."

Eva shook the tow-truck driver's hand gingerly. "I'm Eva and this is Tania," she said. "We're glad to see you," she added politely.

"Most people are," said Steve, grinning and giving Eva a wink. "Especially if they're going nowhere." He pointed to the sign on the back of his truck.

Going Nowhere?
Stick with Steve.

3 A Quiet Little Town

"This really is nowhere," whispered Eva to Tania. The three of them were squeezed uncomfortably into the front of Steve's truck, which was pulling into his garage.

The garage was on the main street of the little town. There were a few other shops and some boarded up buildings. A handful of roads, bordered by clusters of quaint cottages, turned off the main street. There was a park and a war memorial, and a tiny school.

Steve jumped out of the cab and started fiddling with some levers on the tray of the truck. A metal drum at the back whirred noisily, and the chains holding Eva's car slowly clunked to the ground.

"Is there a qualified mechanic here?" asked Eva.

"Sure is," replied Steve. "That would be me."

"You're a mechanic, too?" said Tania, jumping out of the truck.

Steve's
AUTO R

"And an engineer, a registered builder and a real-estate salesman," he said proudly. "Not much call for that last one around here," he added ruefully. "Last place we sold here was in 1986. Or was it 1987?"

Eva laughed. "Really? I would have thought there would be plenty of people wanting a quiet life in the countryside. And it is a pretty town."

Tania looked at her mother. It was a pretty town, in a rundown, forgotten kind of way. The gardens were well-tended, and all the buildings appeared to be in good condition, even the boarded-up ones. Clearly the people who did live here cared for their town.

"Anyway," said Steve, "this qualified mechanic will require an hour or two to figure out what's up with your car. Why don't you wander down to the information centre and do some sightseeing?"

"The information centre," said Eva. "Which way is that?"

Steve winked at her. "Just kidding. That would be me, too."

Eva couldn't help but smile. "Come on, Tania," she said. "We set out to do some exploring, so that's exactly what we'll do."

They headed towards the park, stopping to buy a snack at the small grocery store that doubled as a bakery and a butcher shop.

"What kind of coffees do you have?" asked Eva, noticing that the shop had a few tables outside for people to sit at.

The shopkeeper, whose name tag said "Myrtle", bustled around behind the counter. "Black or white, dear," she said.

Eva smiled. "I'd love a white coffee, thanks. And we'll have a couple of those vanilla slices, too."

"These look delicious," exclaimed Tania, taking a mouthful of vanilla slice.

"They're not bad, are they?" agreed Eva. "And the coffee's quite good."

They sat at a table out on the pavement, watching the world go by. Hardly any cars drove along the street. Someone walked past, saying hello. Eva looked over her shoulder to see if there was someone else behind her, then realised that the stranger was saying hello to her.

"Hello," she replied with a smile. That never happened in the city.

Eva sipped her coffee and relaxed in her chair.

"It really is very peaceful here, isn't it," she commented. "Being stuck in the middle of nowhere isn't nearly as bad as I thought it would be."

"I like it," replied Tania. "It's nice."

Eva went back inside to pay for the coffee and cakes and stopped suddenly.

"Oh, no," she said to the shopkeeper. "I've left my shoulder bag in my car. Oh, how embarrassing!"

"Don't worry," said Myrtle, who was busy rearranging packets on the shelf. "Just pop back and, if I'm not about, leave the money on the counter."

Eva couldn't believe it. That never happened in the city either.

Tania ran down to the park, with Eva close behind. There wasn't a colourful jungle gym or an impressive, twisting slide. There was just an old swing and a faded see-saw, but that was more than enough to keep Tania occupied while Eva sat on the park bench.

She thought about all the people back in the city who would still be leading their chaotic, stressful lifestyle, even on Saturdays. And she looked back at the quiet little town behind her.

"It is nice," thought Eva. "And I like it, too."

Another peaceful hour slipped by without them noticing, and soon it was time for Eva and Tania to make their way back to Steve's garage. On the way,

Eva saw some letters, carved in stone, above an impressive boarded-up building.

"The Empire," she read. She peered through one of the windows and, between the boards, saw an old noticeboard in the gloom.

"Now Showing!" she read out loud. "*Crocodile Dundee.*" She shook her head and looked at Tania. "It's an old movie theatre. And that movie came out in 1986!"

"Yep," said Steve, when they arrived at the garage and asked him about the old theatre. "It was a real shame when the Empire closed its doors. It used to be such a popular spot." He closed the bonnet of Eva's car. "I reckon every family in town used to look forward to Saturday nights there. Popcorn, ice-cream and a good, entertaining movie. Closed down because the company that owned it was opening a multiplex fifty kilometres away. Thought folks would go there instead."

"And did they?" asked Eva, hoping it wasn't her company.

"Nope," said Steve. "Just wasn't the same." He wiped his oily hands on his overalls. "Anyway, your car's fixed. Guess you're itching to head back to the city now."

"Not really," sighed Eva. "But I guess we have to."

"Well, if you ever get stuck again, just give me a call," said Steve. "Stick with Steve. You don't want just anybody towing you out of trouble."

It was a long and silent drive back towards the city.

"Are you OK, Mum?" asked Tania. "You're awfully quiet."

"Yes, I'm fine," said Eva. "I'm just thinking."

After a couple of hours, the traffic grew heavier and the roads turned into freeways. Soon, they found themselves back on the outskirts of the city, crawling along the lanes choked with thousands of frustrated drivers, all trying to get home in time for their favourite shows on TV.

"Welcome home," said Eva, as they inched their way towards the apartment block.

"I had a great day, Mum," said Tania, as they swooped into the underground carpark.

"Me too," said Eva. "Me too."

4 Going Nowhere

Inevitably, Monday rolled around, and Eva turned back into an entertainment lawyer. Suit, make-up and hair ready, she slipped her expensive Italian shoes on, which had been drying out on the balcony.

Already the traffic below had slowed to a crawl. Impatient drivers were cutting in and out of lanes, tooting at pedestrians and cyclists who dared get in their way.

Tania was already dressed for school, her bag in the hallway.

"Come on," called Eva. "If we don't get ourselves into that rush-hour traffic, we'll be late."

After dropping Tania off, edging through the congested roads then finding someone else had taken her carpark, Eva finally made it into the office.

She grabbed a drink from the coffee machine and headed for her desk. There, sitting on top of her neat files and legal notes, sat an envelope.

Eva tore it open. It was from her boss, warning her not to miss any more Saturday meetings. She slumped back in her chair and stared dejectedly at the ceiling.

"That's it," Eva said to herself, her steely lawyer's gaze flickering back on her face. She rummaged through her shoulder bag and pulled out a crumpled business card. She picked up the phone and started to dial.

Steve chuckled loudly. "You're not stuck again, are you?" he said into the phone.

"Yes, I am," replied Eva. "I'm stuck and I'm going nowhere."

"Well, you're in luck," said Steve. "You've called the right man for the job. Where are you this time?"

"Oh, I'm at the office," said Eva. "And it's not a tow truck or a qualified mechanic I need."

"Really?" said Steve, puzzled. "What do you need?"

Eva took a deep breath and told Steve exactly what she needed. And when she'd finished there was a long silence on the other end of the line.

"Are you sure?" asked Steve eventually.

"Absolutely," said Eva. "Besides, I have to come back. I forgot to pay Myrtle for two vanilla slices and a coffee."

The rest of the week raced by. Eva didn't even mind when her regular Friday flights to Sydney and back were as dreadful as she'd expected them to be. During the flights, she sat in the middle seat of her row, not even bothering to jostle elbows with the businessmen on either side. Her mind was elsewhere. She couldn't wait for Saturday morning.

Tania had been looking forward to Saturday all week, too. When Eva had told her they were going to head back to the town in the middle of nowhere, she'd been curious.

"I think you quite like that Steve," Tania said.

Eva turned the slightest shade of red. "Nonsense," she said. "When we get there, you'll find out. It's a surprise."

The heavy wooden doors creaked open. Twenty-five years of musty, stale air floated out into the street, and a torn piece of paper fluttered in the breeze. Eva and Tania stared at the incredible layer of dust that had settled everywhere, marvelling at how big cobwebs could get if you left several generations of spiders to work uninterrupted.

"Needs a little work," commented Steve, handing Eva and Tania a torch each. They picked their way carefully across the debris until they reached an ancient mahogany counter. Tania peered at something there, and then laughed.

"Popcorn, large, $1.50," she read. "Ice-creams, 40 cents. With those prices, it sure has been a long time since anyone's bought anything here."

Eva swung her torch beam upwards and looked at the ceiling. She was astounded to see beautifully carved cherubs and goblins, covered in a cloak of grimy cobwebs, smiling back. She turned to Steve.

"We'll take it," she said.

"Are you sure?" said Steve. "Don't you need to talk to a lawyer or something first?"

"Nope," said Eva. "I've been talking to myself all week."

"Our very own movie theatre," said Tania, who still couldn't believe it. When Eva had outlined her plan on the drive out to the country, Tania had thought she'd finally gone mad with the stress of her job. Then, as Eva explained more and more about her idea, Tania had listened carefully.

"It'll mean a big change for both of us," said Eva. "A change in schools, a change in jobs, a change in where we live. Do you think we could manage that?"

"We would spend more time together," said Tania hopefully.

"Definitely," agreed Eva. "A complete change in lifestyle. What do you say?"

"I haven't done this since 1986. Or 1987," winked Steve. He cleared his workbench in the garage of oily tools and pieces of old engines, and spread out the pages of a real-estate agreement.

"Sign here. And here," he said.

Eva did. And that was it. Eva, Tania and the Empire Theatre had begun a new chapter in their lives.

It took weeks of hard work before the last of the cobwebs had been prised free of their corners. A quarter of a century of grime covered the rows of old red leather seats in the theatre, but with Steve's help, Eva and Tania had finally scrubbed and polished the last seat in the back row. Steve brought in a machine he said he used for steam cleaning the inside of old wrecked cars before doing them up.

That worked a treat on the old carpet, which was transformed from a dull, muddy brown to a vibrant, deep red.

Counters were wiped clean, boards taken down, lightbulbs replaced and cobwebs removed. Slowly, one day at a time, the old Empire started to reveal its old glory.

Word spread throughout the town, and Eva and Tania soon found they had many willing helpers. Myrtle, from the shop, knew just about everyone and, in return for vanilla slices and ample cups of coffee, she assembled enthusiastic working bees almost every afternoon.

5 The Big Day Approaches

Eva met with Mrs Cowan, Tania's new teacher. "We need posters, signs and a colourful mural, right across the front wall," she explained. "Do you think the kids could help us design something?"

She phoned her movie contacts, from her old life in the city. "I need good family movies," she said. "Not the latest blockbusters. Just good, old-fashioned movies that kids and their families can enjoy together. Can you do me a deal?"

She took Myrtle aside and pointed to the mahogany counter, shining under a new coat of varnish and layers of polish.

"I need someone to look after popcorn, ice-cream and drinks," she said. "And I think we could double your sales of vanilla slices," she added with a wink. "Do you think you could manage the snack bar?"

"Goodness," said Myrtle. "Another branch of the shop! I've become a chain."

At the end of one long day of work, Eva and Tania flopped down onto the couch in the little cottage Steve had found for them.

Eva flicked through her messages. Her smart suit, Italian shoes and shoulder bag had been swapped for jeans, trainers and a toolbox, but she still had her mobile phone. Some things, thought Tania, would never change.

Eva had text messages from the bank, the movie company and the regional council.

"Approved," she read aloud to Tania. "Approved. Approved. Approved!"

"Sounds like we're ready to roll!" said Tania excitedly.

"We sure are," beamed Eva.

As the big day approached, the front of the Empire Theatre became mysteriously shrouded in tarpaulins.

"They're the cleanest ones I could find," said Steve, noticing Eva poking at a particularly large oil stain. "And it had better not rain, or my magnificent collection of rusting old car bodies out the back of the garage will become even rustier," he added.

"I'm very grateful, Steve," said Eva. "And even more grateful to your neighbours for putting up with their new view of the wreckers yard out the back."

"Wreckers yard? Priceless relics of our motoring history, more like," said Steve, pretending to sound hurt.

Before she could retort, Eva spotted Mrs Cowan, Tania and a dozen other students from the school heading up the main street.

She pulled back the corner of one of the tarpaulins. "Here you go," she said, smiling at Mrs Cowan. "There should be plenty of room to work back here. Have fun," she said, as the collection of eager faces disappeared behind the canvas.

At last, the Saturday of the Empire Theatre's long-awaited grand re-opening arrived. Tania leapt out of bed to find Eva already up with a cup of coffee out in the garden. She was pacing around nervously.

"Is everything OK, Mum?" asked Tania.

"Yes, dear," replied Eva. "I'm just anxious about tonight. What if we haven't thought of everything? What if nobody turns up?"

"I don't think you need to worry," Tania reassured her. "The posters we made at school are in every window along the main street. Just about everyone in town has been involved in repainting, repolishing and repairing something in the Empire. Of course they'll come."

"I hope so," said Eva.

"Besides," said Tania, "Steve and I will definitely be there. Between the three of us, I'm sure we can polish off Myrtle's vanilla slices."

Eva laughed.

"And don't worry, Mum," added Tania mischievously. "I'll make sure I don't sit between you and Steve."

Eva's face turned the slightest shade of red again.

Five o'clock finally crawled around, after a day that seemed as long as a week of wet Sundays.

"Eva Schiavoni, entertainment mogul, ready for action!" declared Eva as she strode out of her bedroom. "How do I look?"

With her smart suit, careful make-up, perfectly styled hair and confident manner, Tania's mother looked every bit like she used to in the city, when she was heading off to work. But there was one important change. Instead of a steely gaze, she wore a broad smile on her face.

"You look great, Mum," said Tania. "Shall we go? We don't want to get caught in the traffic jam."

6 A Grand Opening

Tania had been joking, of course. But when she and Eva turned the corner of their street and stared down the main road, they couldn't believe their eyes. They were astounded to see that there really was a traffic jam.

Every parking space along the normally quiet main road was taken, and a crowd of excited movie-goers was lined up outside the Empire.

"It's exactly like the city on a Saturday evening," giggled Eva. "I thought we'd left all this behind." She half expected to hear a helicopter thumping its way overhead. Instead, the noise of the traffic and the crowd was drowned out by the crunching of gears and the tooting of a horn, as Steve's tow truck made its way towards the theatre.

"What have you got on the back of the truck?" asked Eva, when she and Tania managed to make it through the crowd of people.

"You'll see," replied Steve. "If you're going nowhere, stick with Steve and you'll go there in style."

"Welcome to the grand opening of the new Empire Theatre," said Eva, addressing the crowd from atop a wooden box outside the theatre doors. "Instead of cutting a ribbon, we have something much more special." Eva turned to the tarpaulins that still covered the wall of the theatre, then tugged on a rope.

The tarpaulins parted to reveal the Empire Theatre looking as proud as it did the day it opened the first time. The crowd clapped and cheered, as they admired the mural of a line of happy movie-goers that ran around the bottom of the wall.

"That's you, Dad," called out one of the students proudly.

"And that's my brother and sister," called out another, pointing at the mural.

"And there's my granddad," piped up another student.

Just about everyone in the town found a portrait

of themselves on the theatre wall. The children had designed a mural that made everyone in the town feel like a part of the new Empire Theatre – literally!

"I declare the new Empire Theatre officially open!" shouted Eva, waving towards the doors.

"Hold on!" came Steve's voice from behind the crowd. There was a gnashing of gears and, to everyone's surprise, he carefully reversed his truck through the crowd and towards the doors.

He jumped out of the cab and ran to the rear of the truck. He fiddled with some levers and the drum on the back of the truck started to move.

But instead of chains clanking down, Eva saw that a wide strip of red carpet was slowly unwinding from the drum.

"Where on earth ..." gasped Eva in amazement.

"The Governor-General came here to open the school in 1965. Or was it 1965?" said Steve.

"1965," replied Myrtle, who was holding one of the theatre doors open. "He ate three entire vanilla slices. I remember it quite clearly."

The crowd proudly paraded up the red carpet and into the foyer of the Empire.

They bought popcorn and ice-creams and vanilla slices from Myrtle's new branch, as she called it. They found their seats, and waited eagerly for the show to start.

Soon, there was just Steve, Eva, Tania and Myrtle out in the foyer.

"Come on, Mum, we'll miss the trailers," said Tania.

"Hold on a minute, dear," called Myrtle from behind the counter. There was a lot of steam and hissing coming from beneath the mahogany, and her glasses had clouded up.

She proudly plonked a paper cup on the counter and smiled at Eva.

"That's for you, dear," she said.

Eva smiled at Myrtle. "Well, thank you, Myrtle, but I ..."

"It's a latte," said Myrtle insistently. "Your Tania taught me how to make it."

Eva hugged Myrtle, who looked surprised. She picked up the cup and hurried back to Steve and Tania.

"It's really only a fancy white coffee," chuckled Myrtle to herself.

“This is it!” said Eva.

“It sure is,” agreed Tania.

The lights in the theatre went down, and they walked to the door, ready to enter.

Steve smiled at Eva and, with a flourish, offered her his arm.

“Going nowhere, madam?” he enquired.

“No,” replied Eva with a smile. “Definitely not.” She took his arm. “But I think I’ll stick with Steve, all the same.”